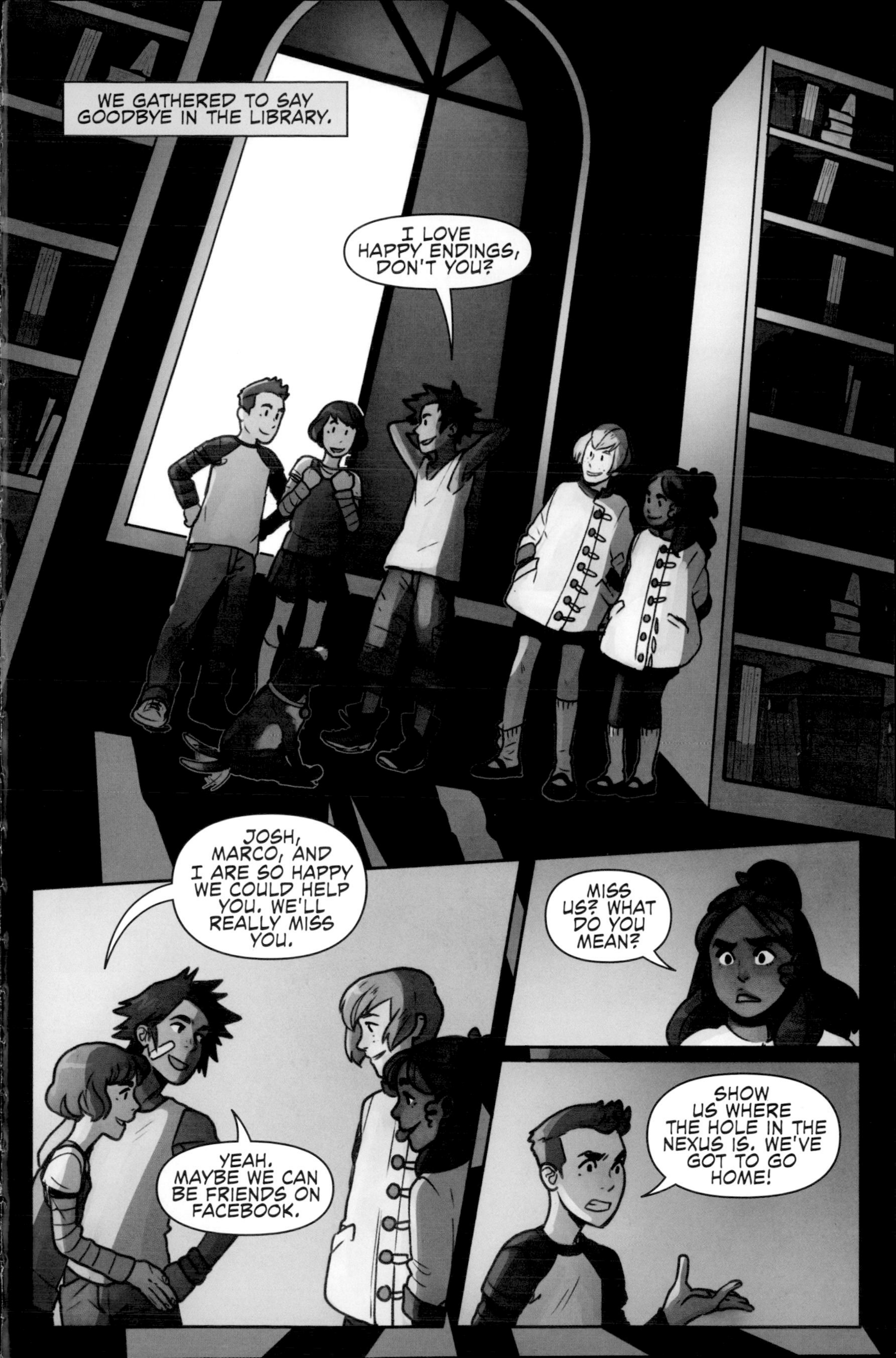
WE GATHERED TO SAY GOODBYE IN THE LIBRARY.
I LOVE HAPPY ENDINGS, DON'T YOU?
JOSH, MARCO, AND I ARE SO HAPPY WE COULD HELP YOU. WE'LL REALLY MISS YOU.
YEAH. MAYBE WE CAN BE FRIENDS ON FACEBOOK.
MISS US? WHAT DO YOU MEAN?
SHOW US WHERE THE HOLE IN THE NEXUS IS. WE'VE GOT TO GO HOME!

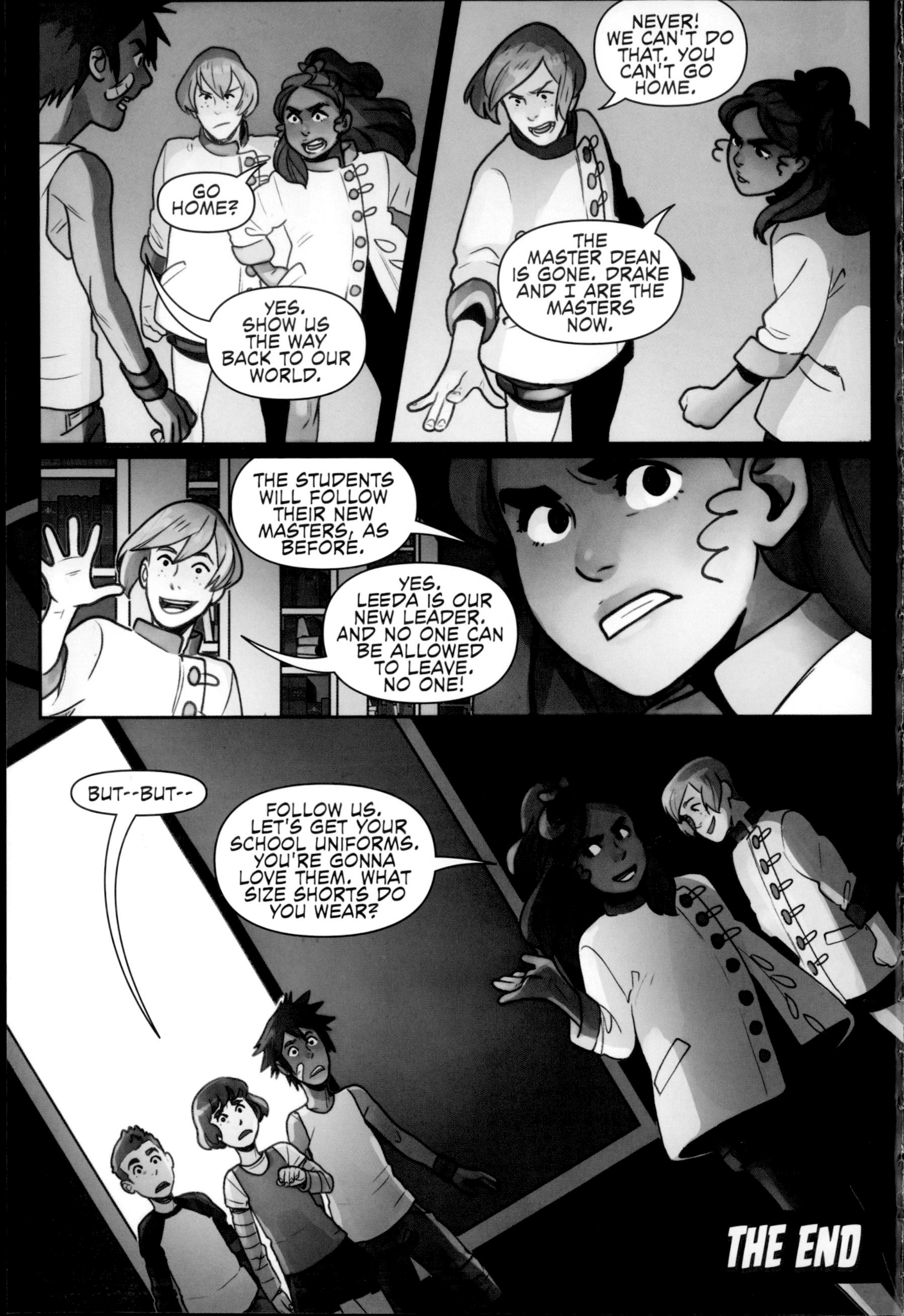
GO HOME?
YES. SHOW US THE WAY BACK TO OUR WORLD.
NEVER! WE CAN'T DO THAT. YOU CAN'T GO HOME.
THE MASTER DEAN IS GONE. DRAKE AND I ARE THE MASTERS NOW.
THE STUDENTS WILL FOLLOW THEIR NEW MASTERS, AS BEFORE.
YES. LEEDA IS OUR NEW LEADER. AND NO ONE CAN BE ALLOWED TO LEAVE. NO ONE!
BUT--BUT--
FOLLOW US. LET'S GET YOUR SCHOOL UNIFORMS. YOU'RE GONNA LOVE THEM. WHAT SIZE SHORTS DO YOU WEAR?
THE END

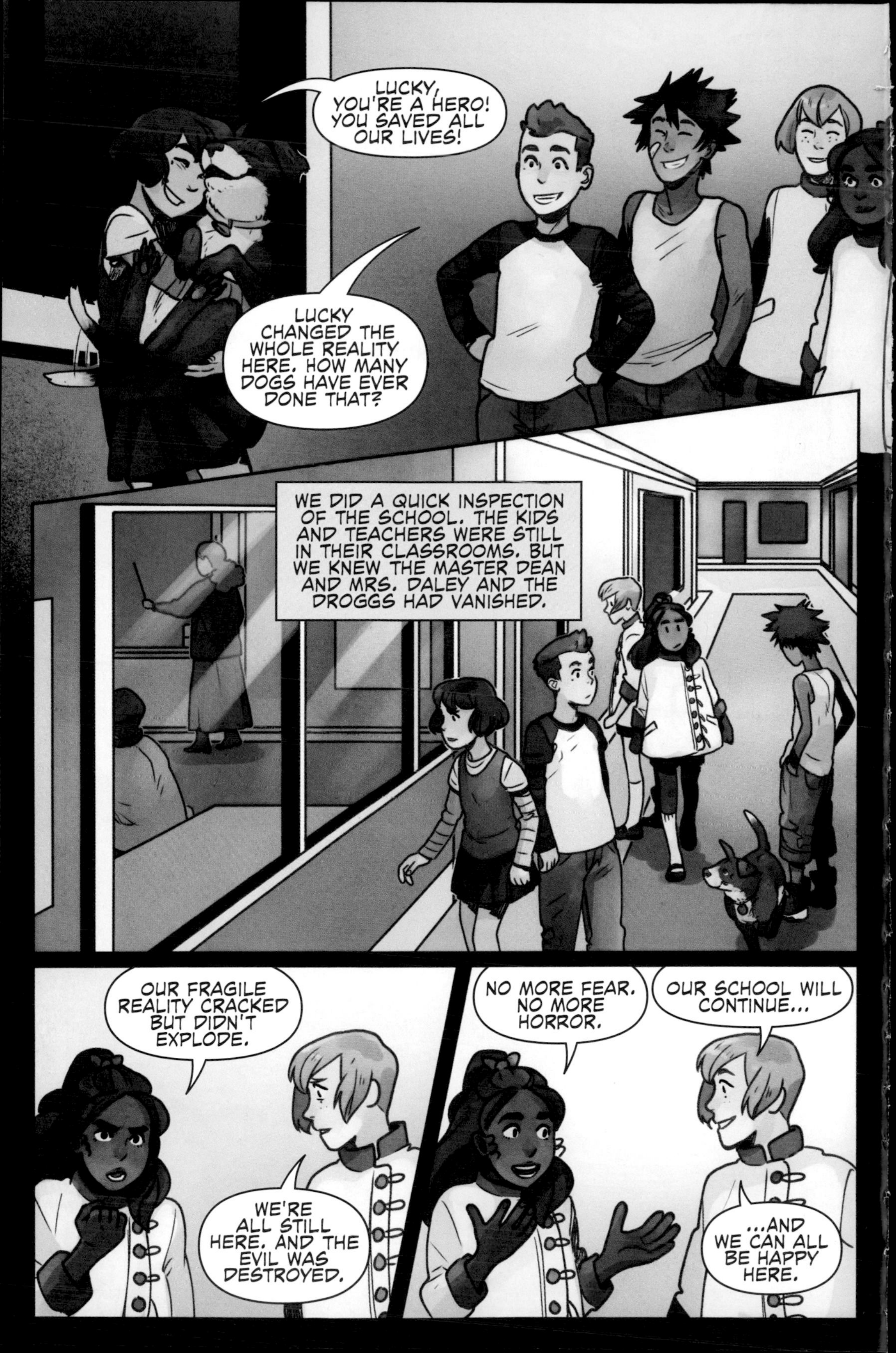
LUCKY, YOU'RE A HERO! YOU SAVED ALL OUR LIVES!
LUCKY CHANGED THE WHOLE REALITY HERE. HOW MANY DOGS HAVE EVER DONE THAT?
WE DID A QUICK INSPECTION OF THE SCHOOL. THE KIDS AND TEACHERS WERE STILL IN THEIR CLASSROOMS. BUT WE KNEW THE MASTER DEAN AND MRS. DALEY AND THE DROGGS HAD VANISHED.
OUR FRAGILE REALITY CRACKED BUT DIDN'T EXPLODE.
WE'RE ALL STILL HERE. AND THE EVIL WAS DESTROYED.
NO MORE FEAR. NO MORE HORROR.
OUR SCHOOL WILL CONTINUE...
...AND WE CAN ALL BE HAPPY HERE.

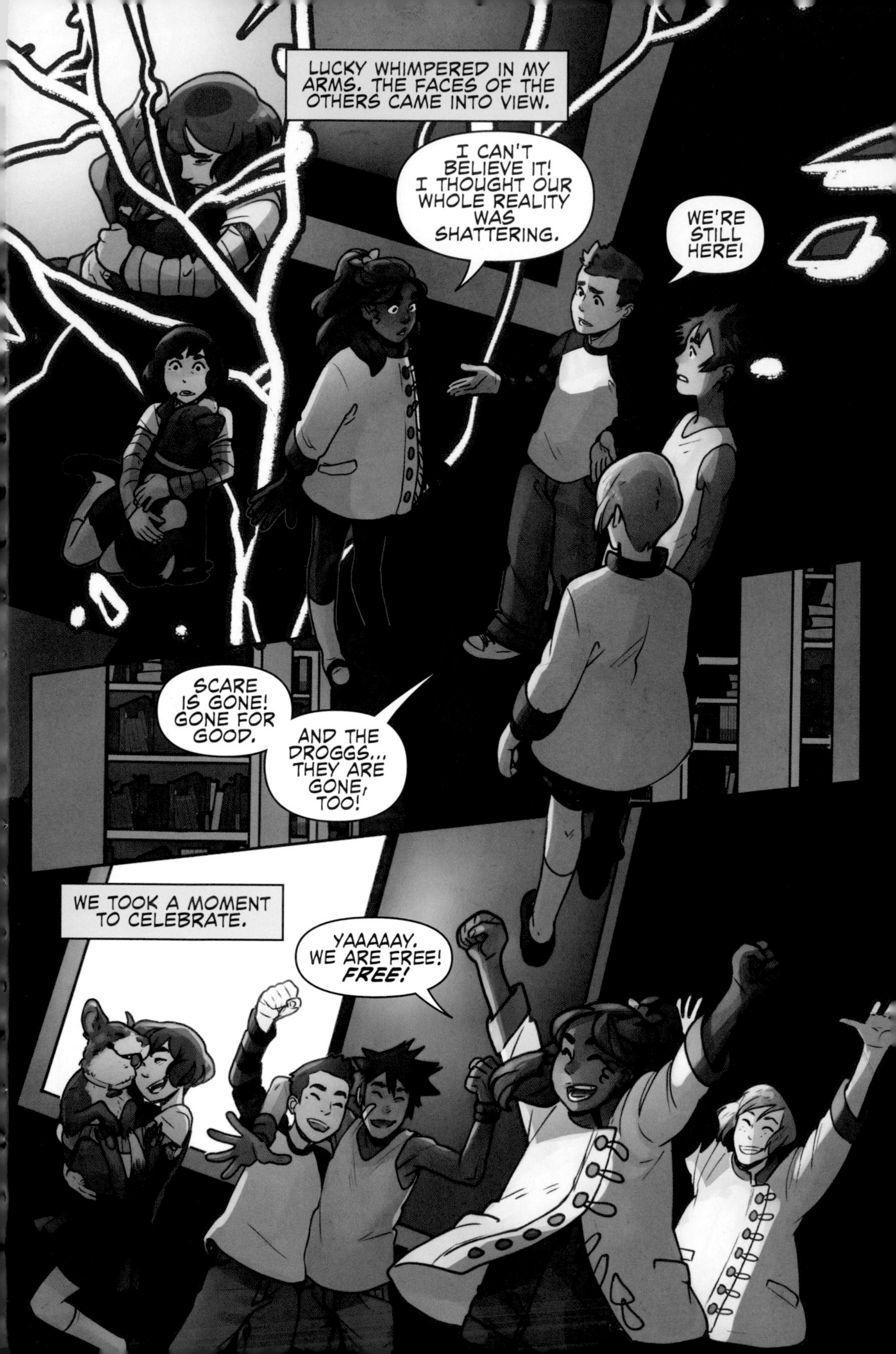
LUCKY WHIMPERED IN MY ARMS. THE FACES OF THE OTHERS CAME INTO VIEW.
I CAN'T BELIEVE IT! I THOUGHT OUR WHOLE REALITY WAS SHATTERING.
WE'RE STILL HERE!
SCARE IS GONE! GONE FOR GOOD.
AND THE DROGGS... THEY ARE GONE, TOO!
WE TOOK A MOMENT TO CELEBRATE.
YAAAAAY. WE ARE FREE! *FREE!*

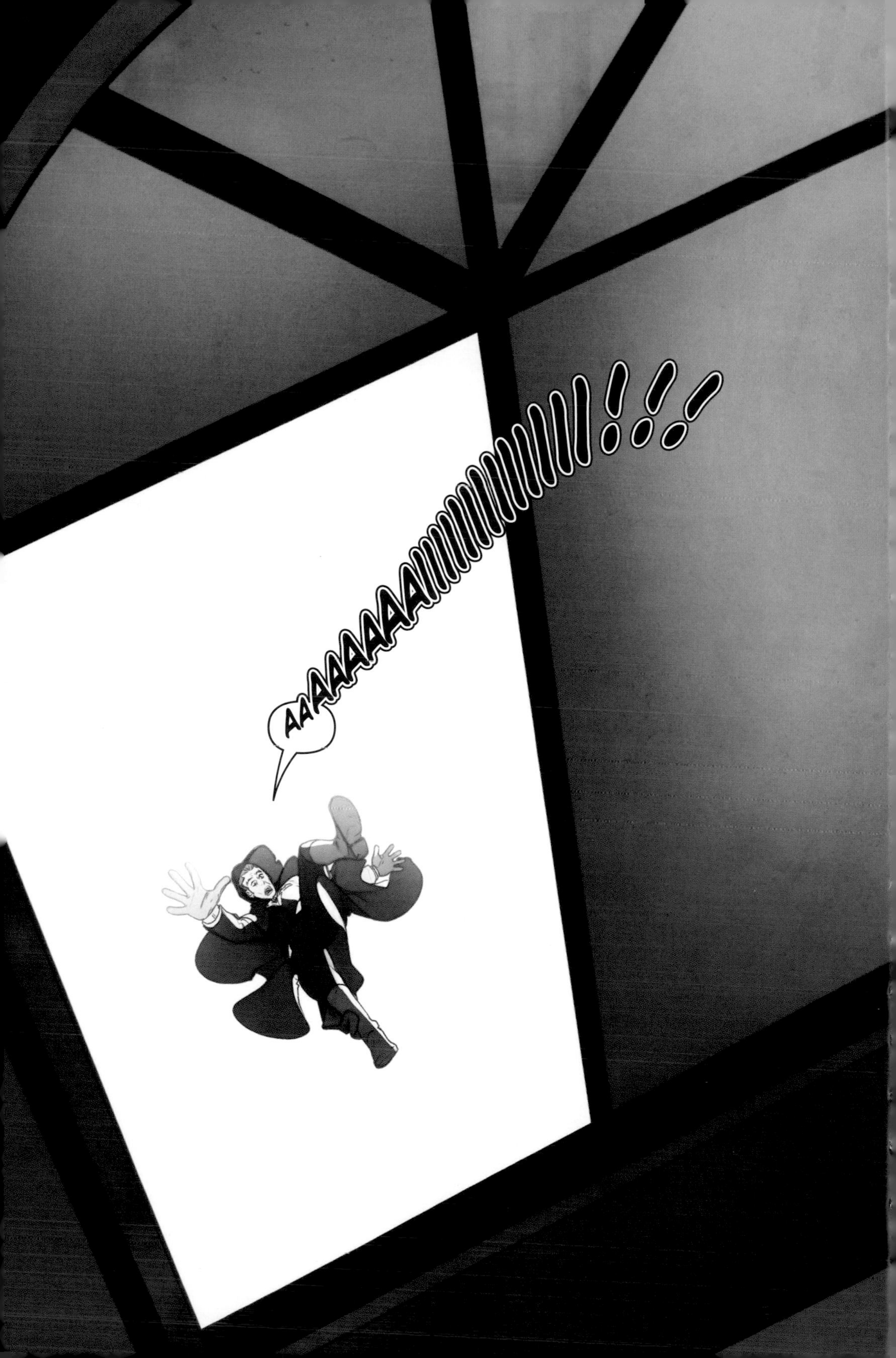
AAAAAAAAAIIIIIIIIIIIIIII!!!

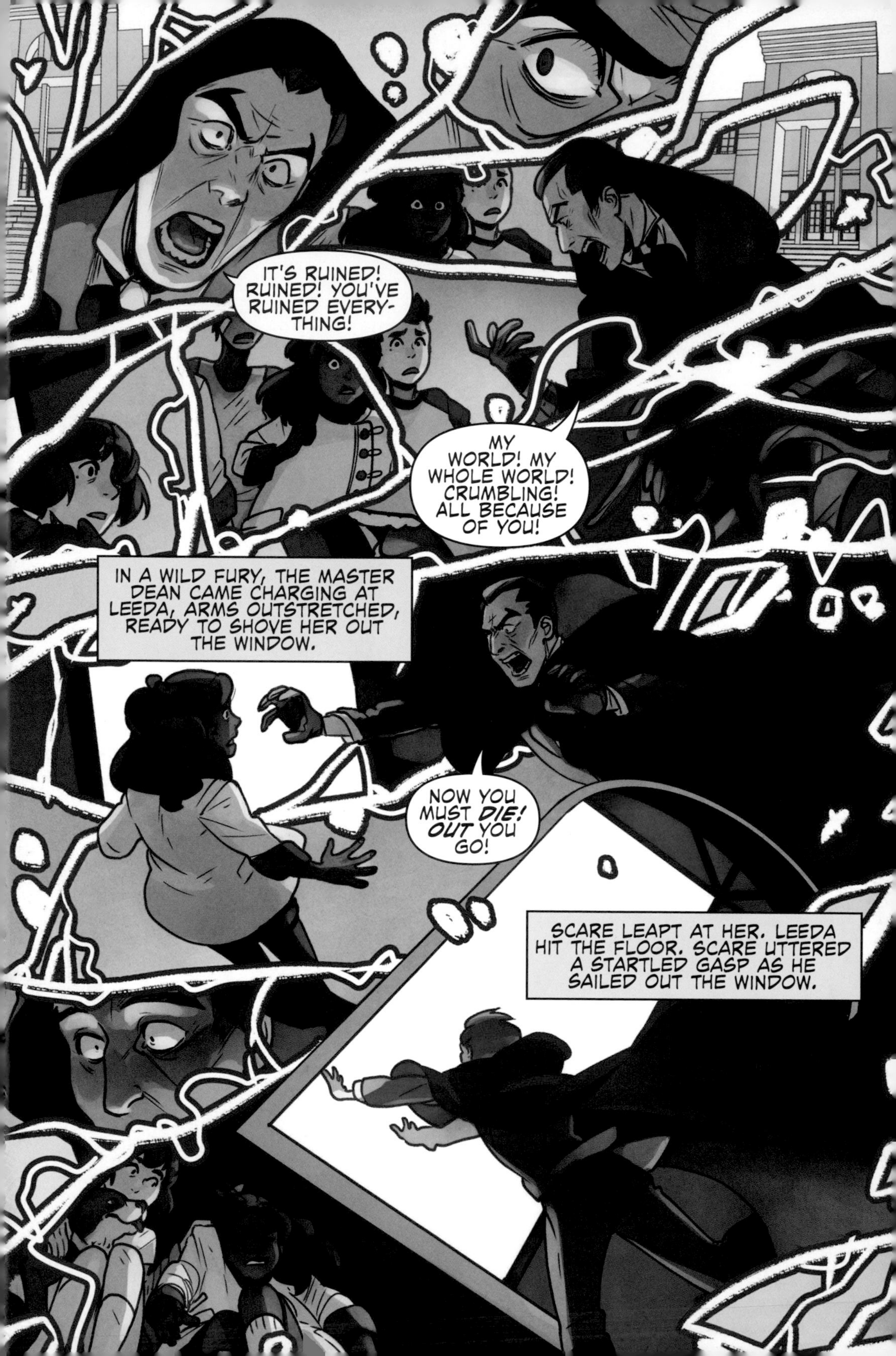
IT'S RUINED! RUINED! YOU'VE RUINED EVERY-THING!
MY WORLD! MY WHOLE WORLD! CRUMBLING! ALL BECAUSE OF YOU!
IN A WILD FURY, THE MASTER DEAN CAME CHARGING AT LEEDA, ARMS OUTSTRETCHED, READY TO SHOVE HER OUT THE WINDOW.
NOW YOU MUST ***DIE! OUT*** YOU GO!
SCARE LEAPT AT HER. LEEDA HIT THE FLOOR. SCARE UTTERED A STARTLED GASP AS HE SAILED OUT THE WINDOW.

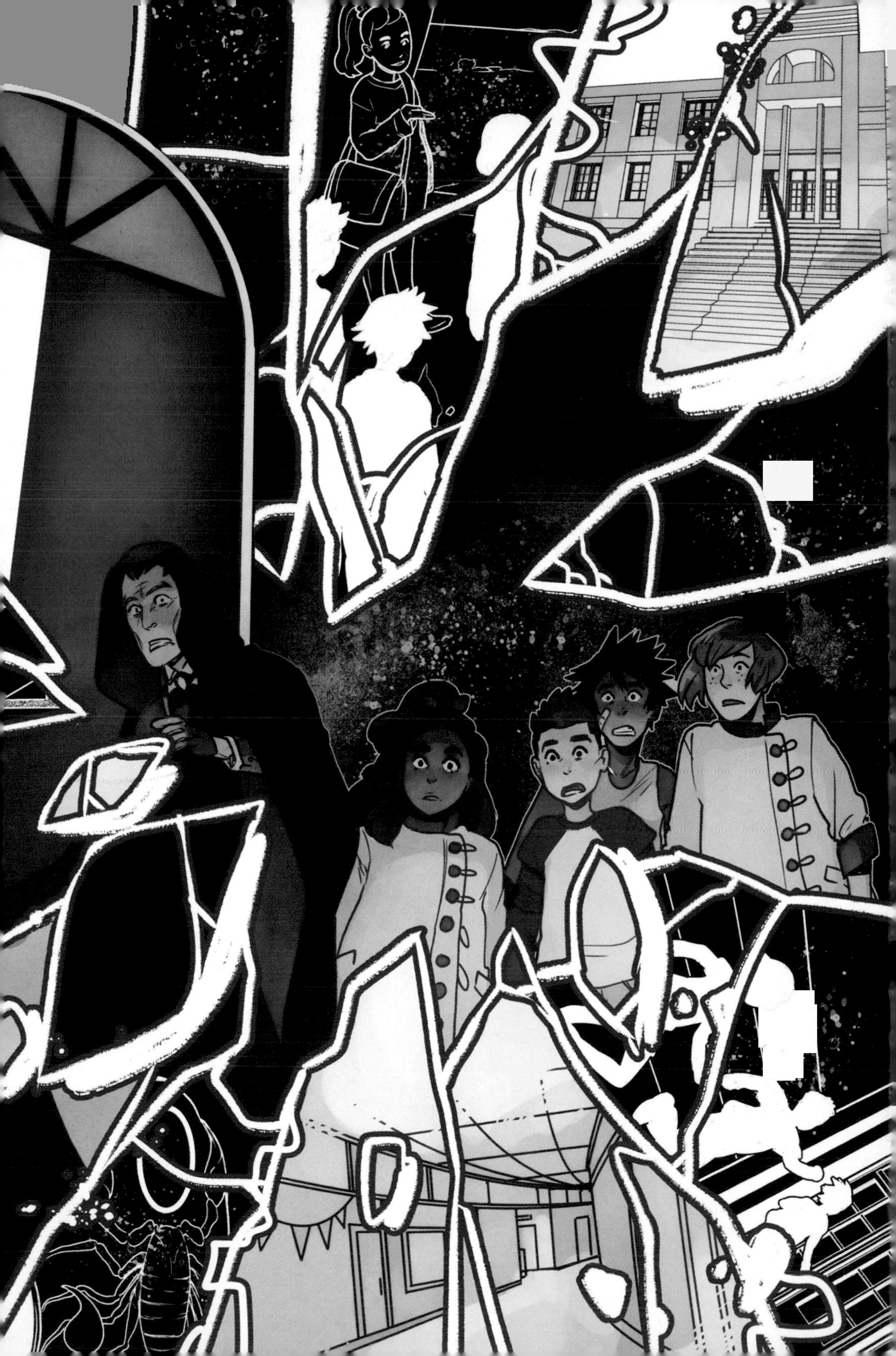

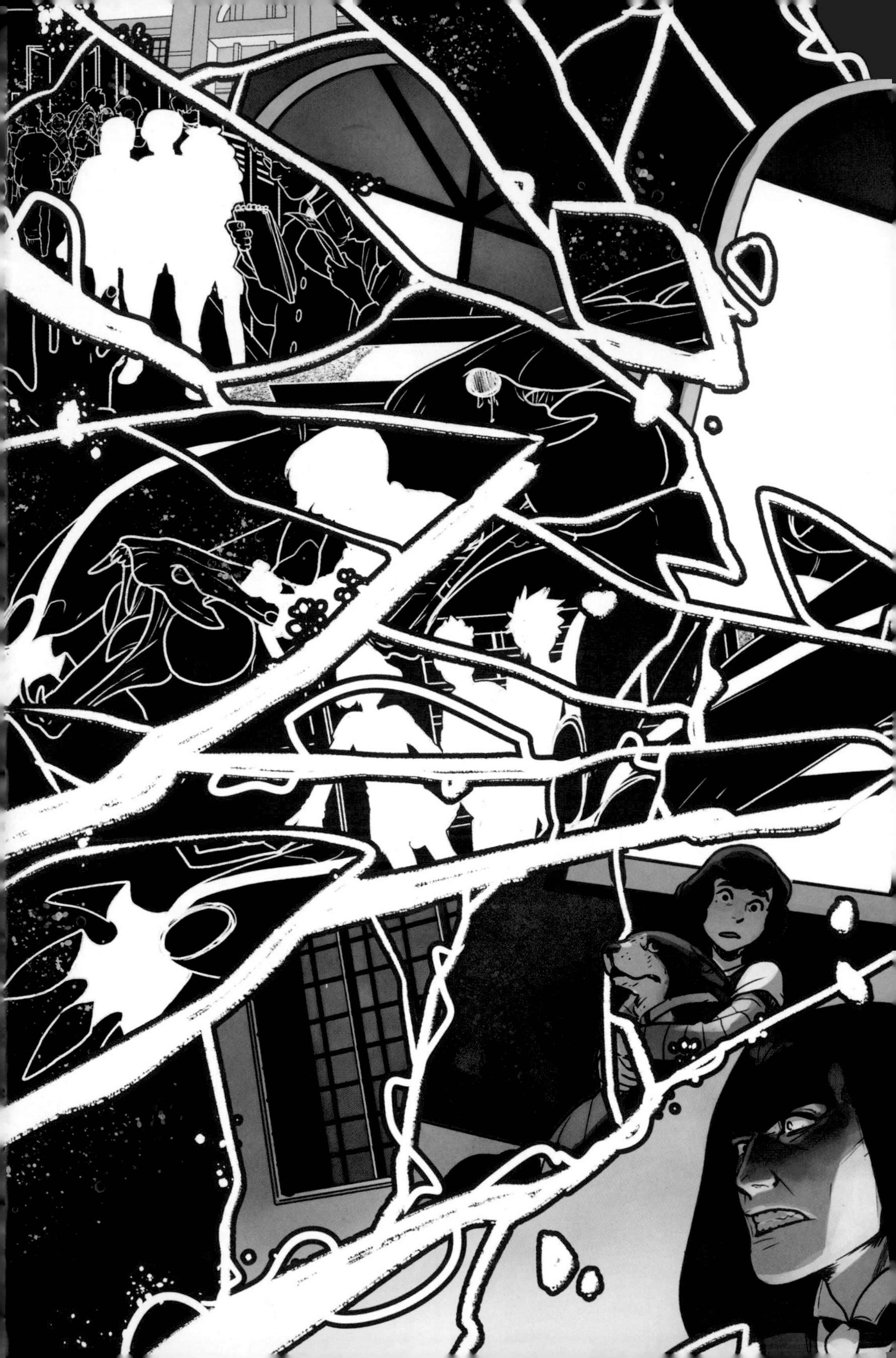

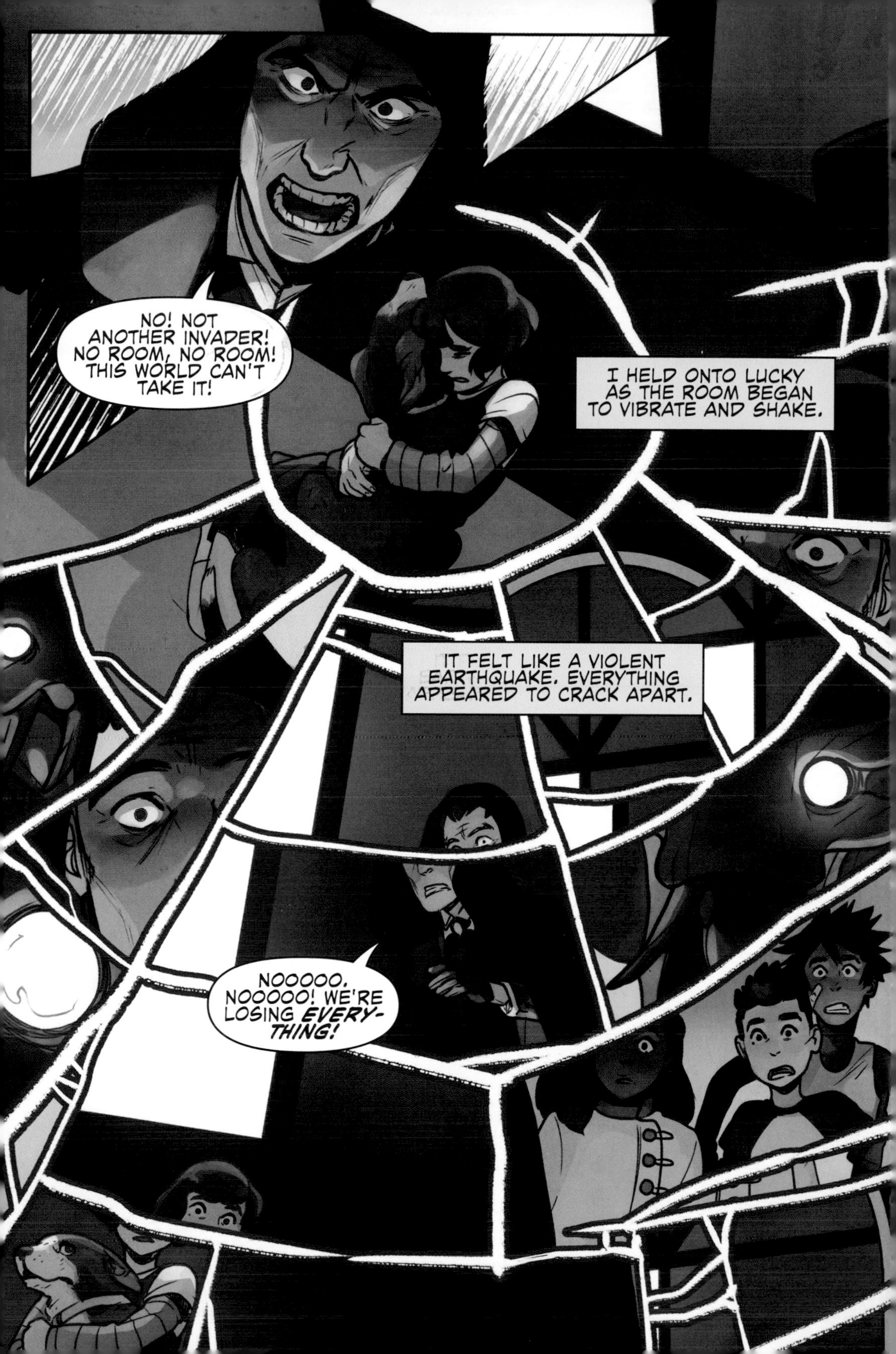
NO! NOT ANOTHER INVADER! NO ROOM, NO ROOM! THIS WORLD CAN'T TAKE IT!
I HELD ONTO LUCKY AS THE ROOM BEGAN TO VIBRATE AND SHAKE.
IT FELT LIKE A VIOLENT EARTHQUAKE. EVERYTHING APPEARED TO CRACK APART.
NOOOOO. NOOOOO! WE'RE LOSING *EVERY-THING!*

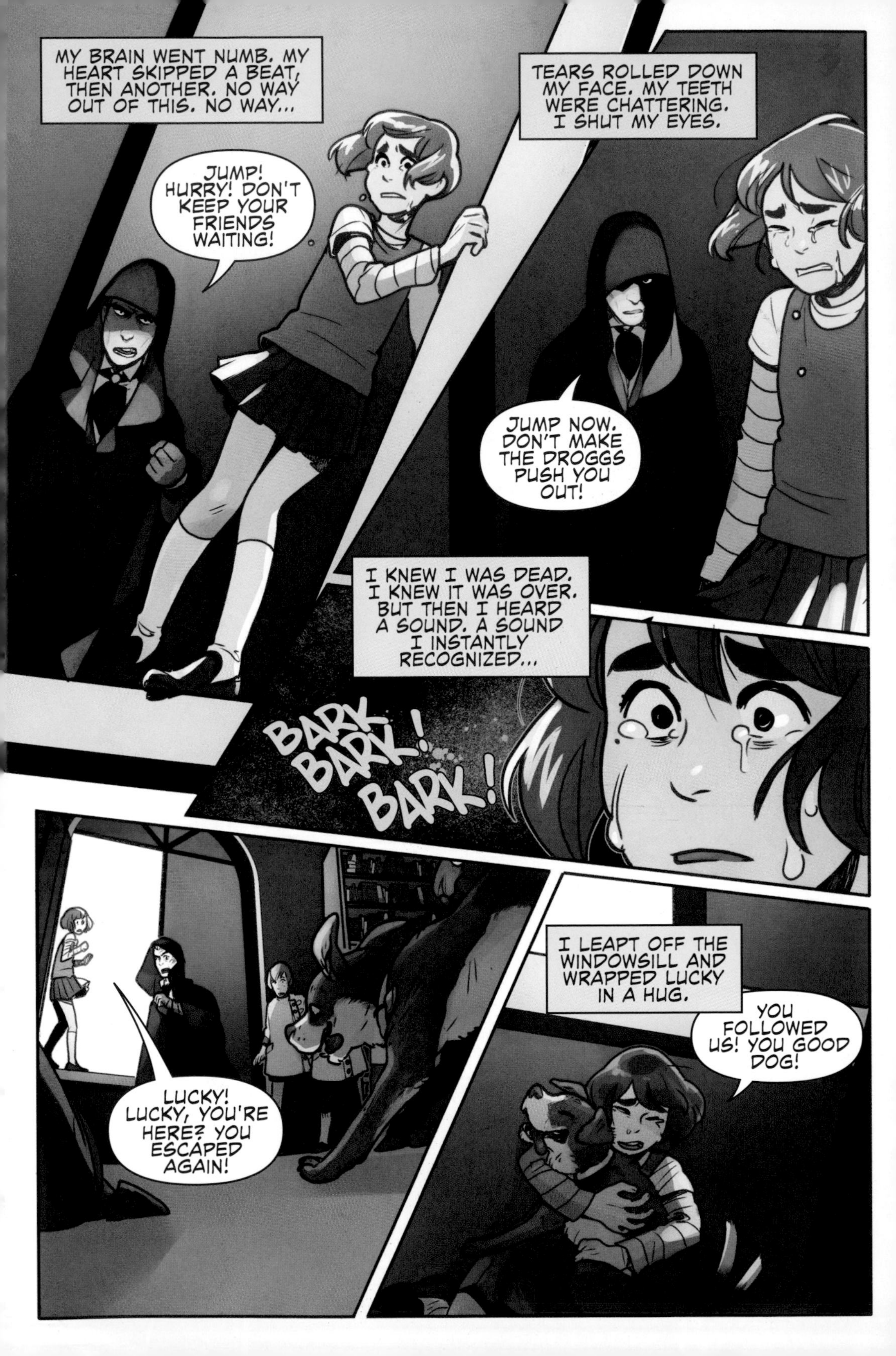
MY BRAIN WENT NUMB. MY HEART SKIPPED A BEAT, THEN ANOTHER. NO WAY OUT OF THIS. NO WAY...
JUMP! HURRY! DON'T KEEP YOUR FRIENDS WAITING!
TEARS ROLLED DOWN MY FACE. MY TEETH WERE CHATTERING. I SHUT MY EYES.
JUMP NOW. DON'T MAKE THE DROGGS PUSH YOU OUT!
I KNEW I WAS DEAD. I KNEW IT WAS OVER. BUT THEN I HEARD A SOUND. A SOUND I INSTANTLY RECOGNIZED...
BARK BARK! BARK!
LUCKY! LUCKY, YOU'RE HERE? YOU ESCAPED AGAIN!
I LEAPT OFF THE WINDOWSILL AND WRAPPED LUCKY IN A HUG.
YOU FOLLOWED US! YOU GOOD DOG!

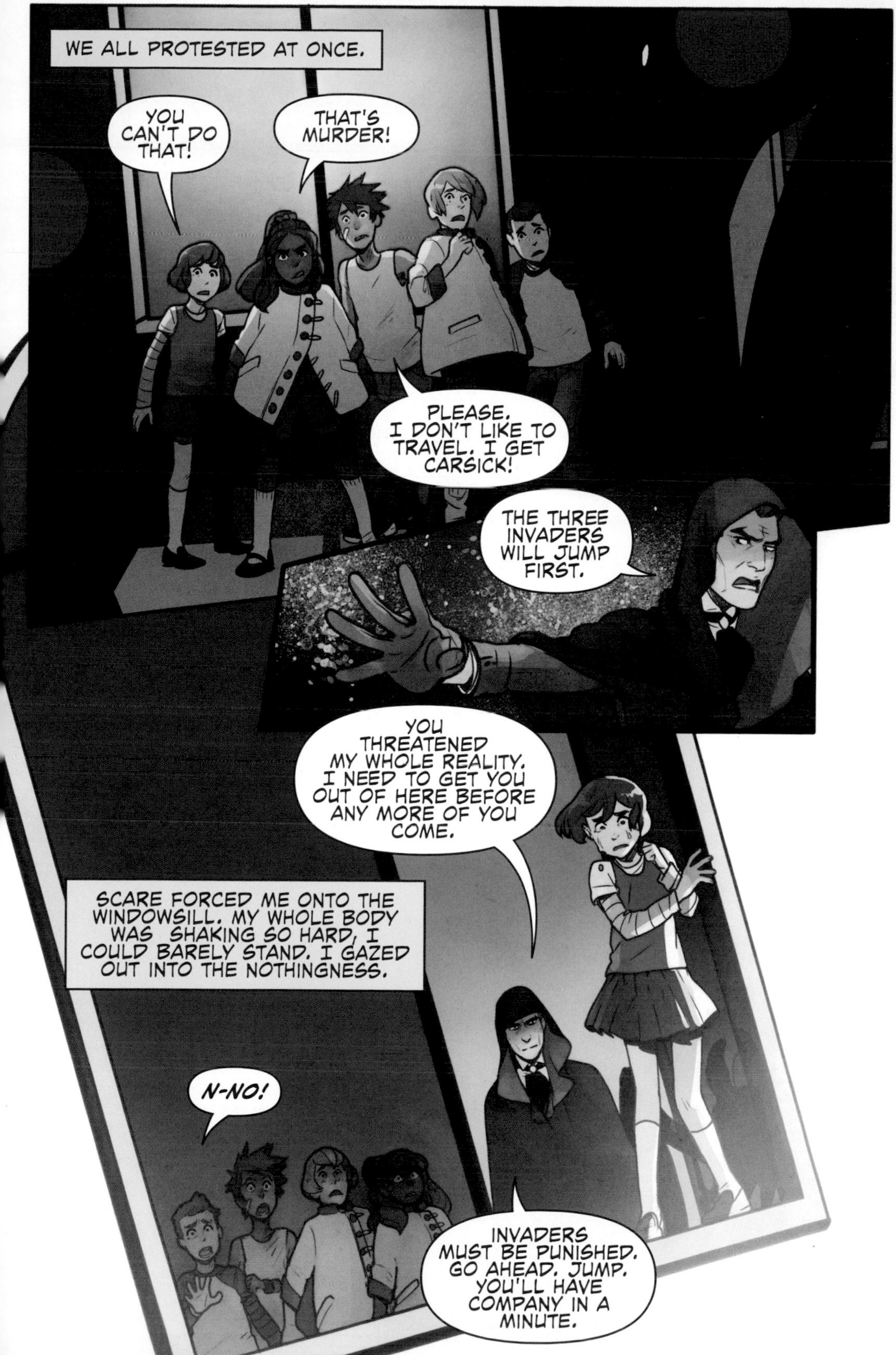
WE ALL PROTESTED AT ONCE.
YOU CAN'T DO THAT!
THAT'S MURDER!
PLEASE. I DON'T LIKE TO TRAVEL. I GET CARSICK!
THE THREE INVADERS WILL JUMP FIRST.
YOU THREATENED MY WHOLE REALITY. I NEED TO GET YOU OUT OF HERE BEFORE ANY MORE OF YOU COME.
SCARE FORCED ME ONTO THE WINDOWSILL. MY WHOLE BODY WAS SHAKING SO HARD, I COULD BARELY STAND. I GAZED OUT INTO THE NOTHINGNESS.
N-NO!
INVADERS MUST BE PUNISHED. GO AHEAD. JUMP. YOU'LL HAVE COMPANY IN A MINUTE.

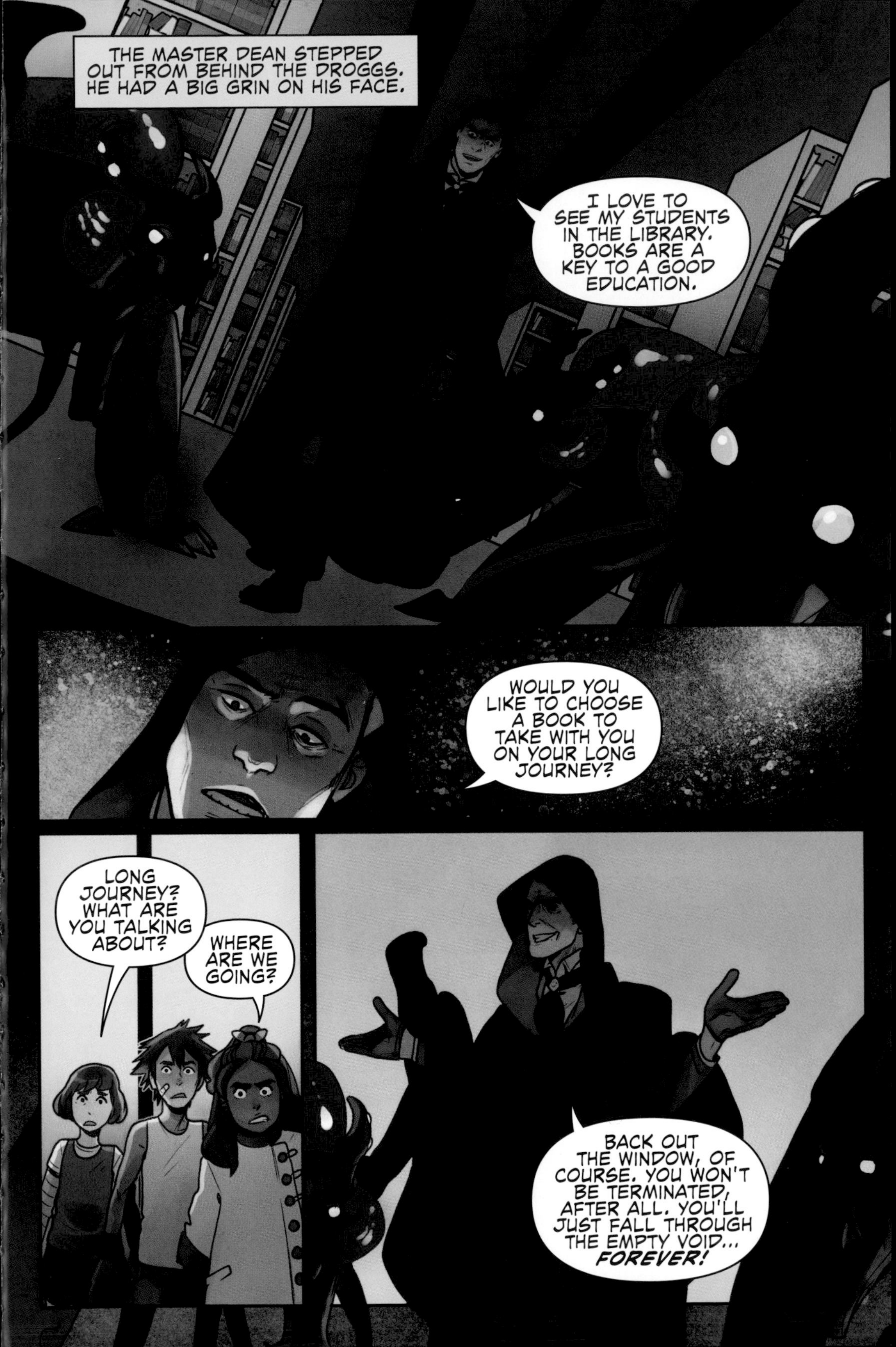
THE MASTER DEAN STEPPED OUT FROM BEHIND THE DROGGS. HE HAD A BIG GRIN ON HIS FACE.
I LOVE TO SEE MY STUDENTS IN THE LIBRARY. BOOKS ARE A KEY TO A GOOD EDUCATION.
WOULD YOU LIKE TO CHOOSE A BOOK TO TAKE WITH YOU ON YOUR LONG JOURNEY?
LONG JOURNEY? WHAT ARE YOU TALKING ABOUT?
WHERE ARE WE GOING?
BACK OUT THE WINDOW, OF COURSE. YOU WON'T BE TERMINATED, AFTER ALL. YOU'LL JUST FALL THROUGH THE EMPTY VOID... ***FOREVER!***

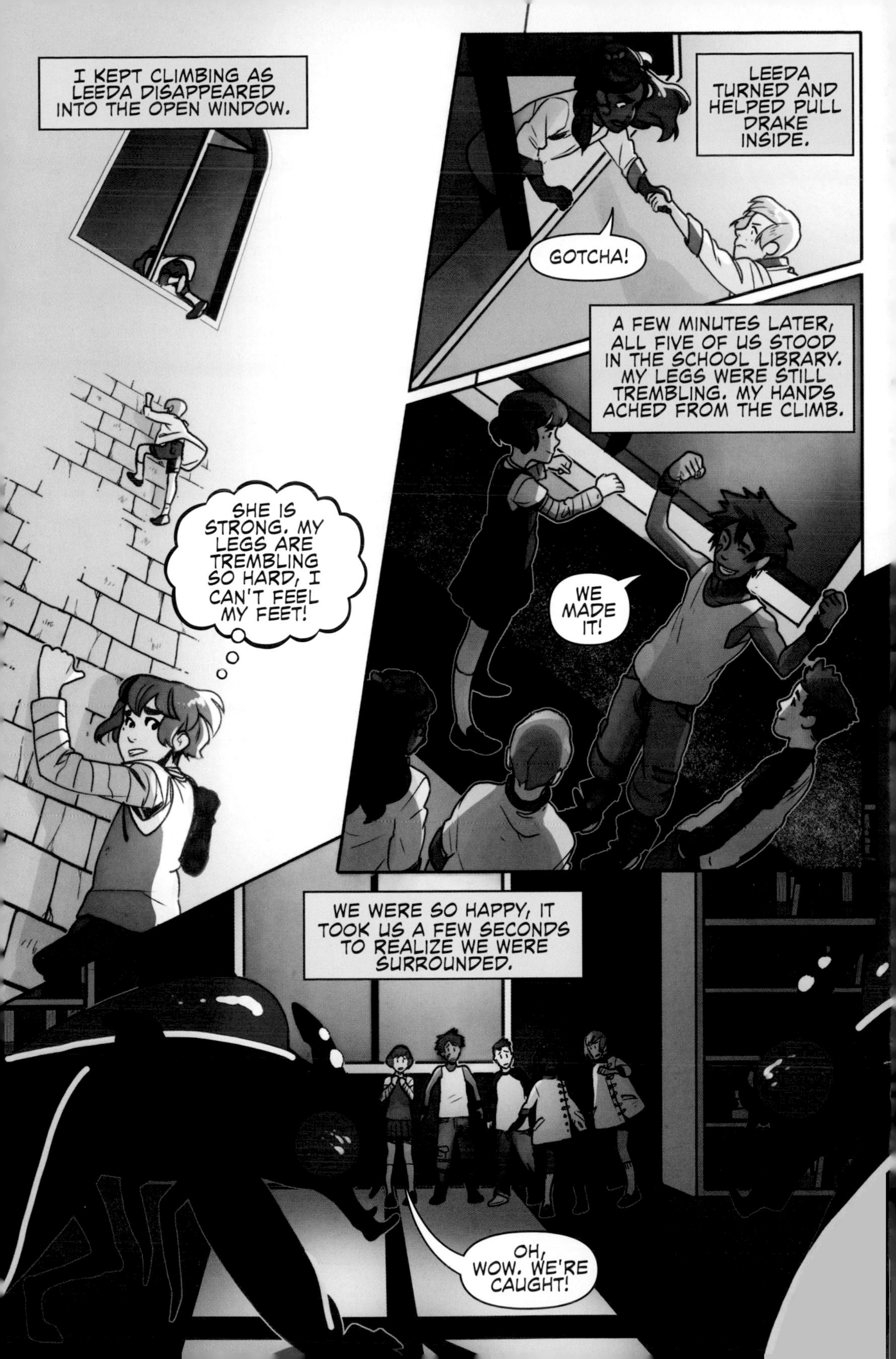
I KEPT CLIMBING AS LEEDA DISAPPEARED INTO THE OPEN WINDOW.
LEEDA TURNED AND HELPED PULL DRAKE INSIDE.
GOTCHA!
SHE IS STRONG. MY LEGS ARE TREMBLING SO HARD, I CAN'T FEEL MY FEET!
A FEW MINUTES LATER, ALL FIVE OF US STOOD IN THE SCHOOL LIBRARY. MY LEGS WERE STILL TREMBLING. MY HANDS ACHED FROM THE CLIMB.
WE MADE IT!
WE WERE SO HAPPY, IT TOOK US A FEW SECONDS TO REALIZE WE WERE SURROUNDED.
OH, WOW. WE'RE CAUGHT!

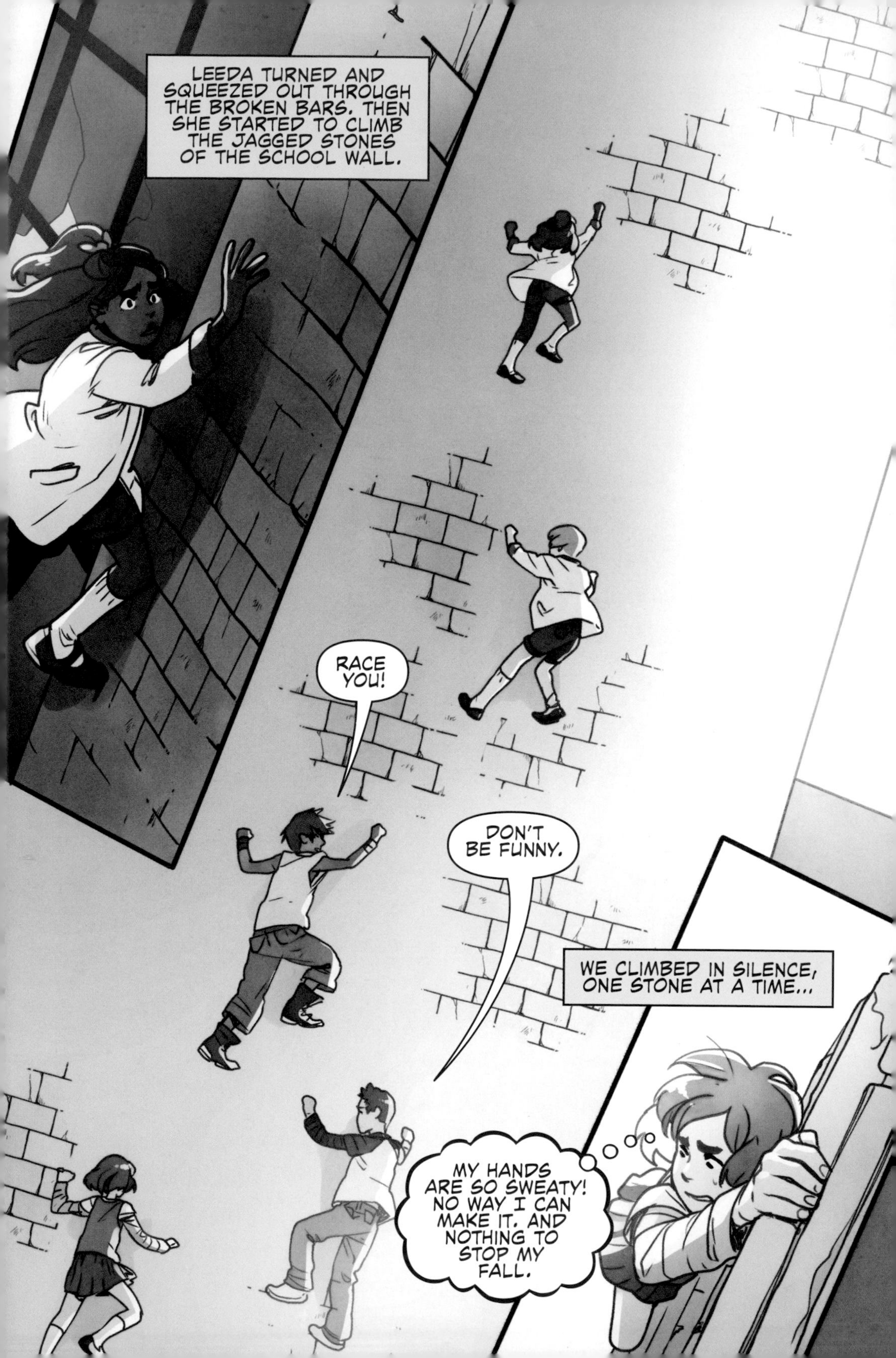
LEEDA TURNED AND SQUEEZED OUT THROUGH THE BROKEN BARS. THEN SHE STARTED TO CLIMB THE JAGGED STONES OF THE SCHOOL WALL.
RACE YOU!
DON'T BE FUNNY.
WE CLIMBED IN SILENCE, ONE STONE AT A TIME...
MY HANDS ARE SO SWEATY! NO WAY I CAN MAKE IT. AND NOTHING TO STOP MY FALL.

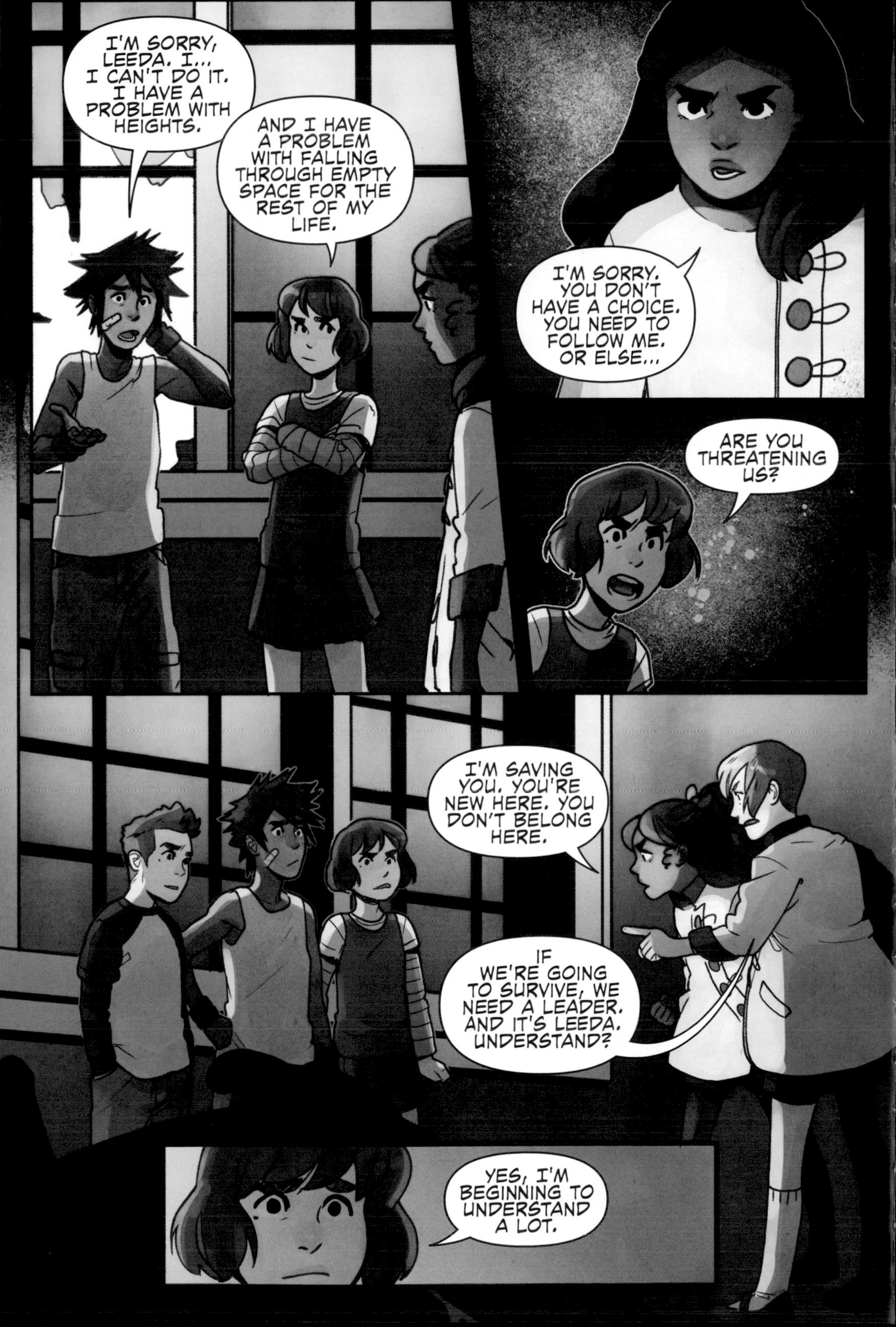
I'M SORRY, LEEDA. I... I CAN'T DO IT. I HAVE A PROBLEM WITH HEIGHTS.
AND I HAVE A PROBLEM WITH FALLING THROUGH EMPTY SPACE FOR THE REST OF MY LIFE.
I'M SORRY. YOU DON'T HAVE A CHOICE. YOU NEED TO FOLLOW ME. OR ELSE...
ARE YOU THREATENING US?
I'M SAVING YOU. YOU'RE NEW HERE. YOU DON'T BELONG HERE.
IF WE'RE GOING TO SURVIVE, WE NEED A LEADER. AND IT'S LEEDA. UNDERSTAND?
YES, I'M BEGINNING TO UNDERSTAND A LOT.

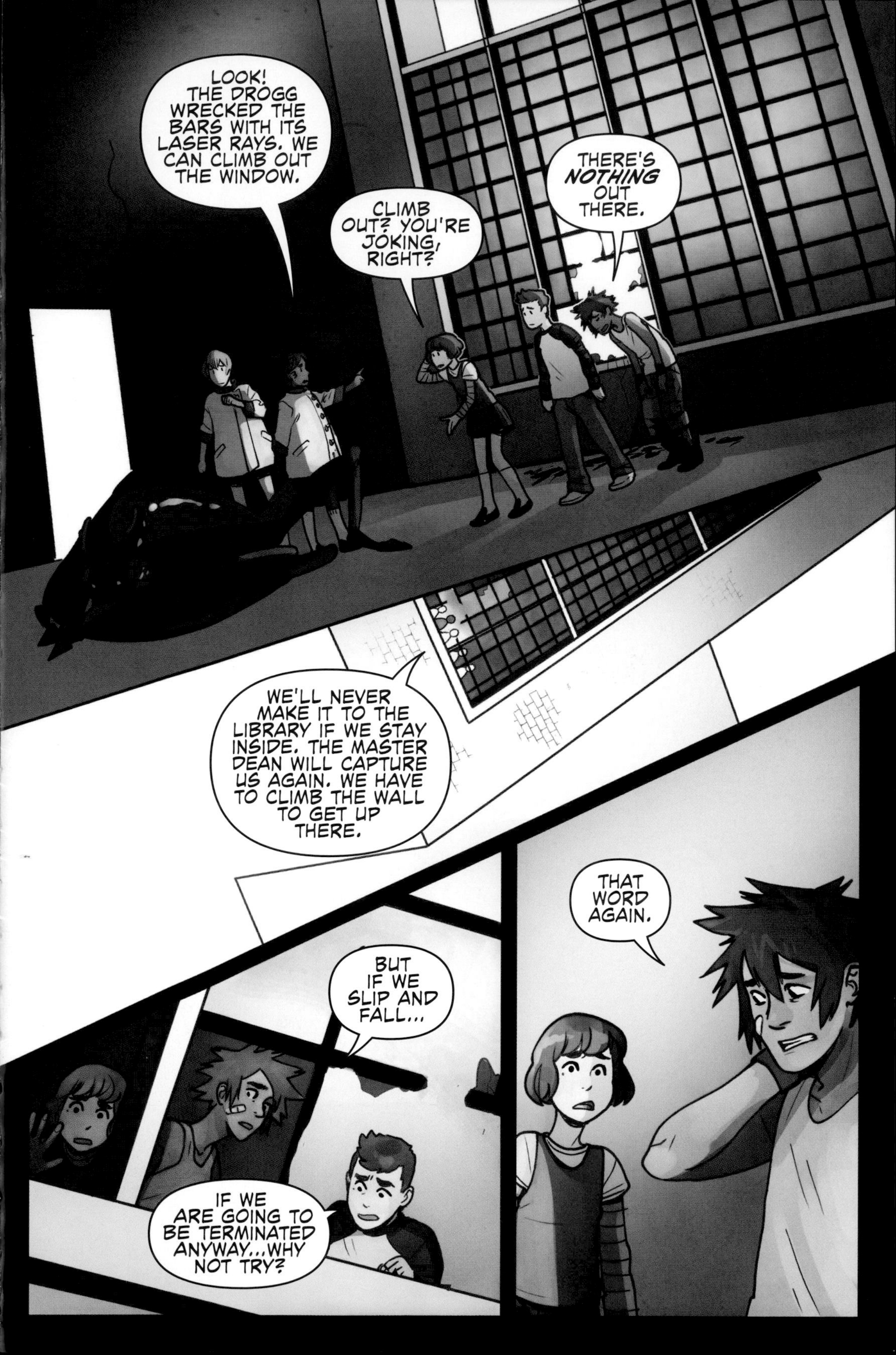
LOOK! THE DROGG WRECKED THE BARS WITH ITS LASER RAYS. WE CAN CLIMB OUT THE WINDOW.
CLIMB OUT? YOU'RE JOKING, RIGHT?
THERE'S NOTHING OUT THERE.
WE'LL NEVER MAKE IT TO THE LIBRARY IF WE STAY INSIDE. THE MASTER DEAN WILL CAPTURE US AGAIN. WE HAVE TO CLIMB THE WALL TO GET UP THERE.
BUT IF WE SLIP AND FALL...
IF WE ARE GOING TO BE TERMINATED ANYWAY...WHY NOT TRY?
THAT WORD AGAIN.

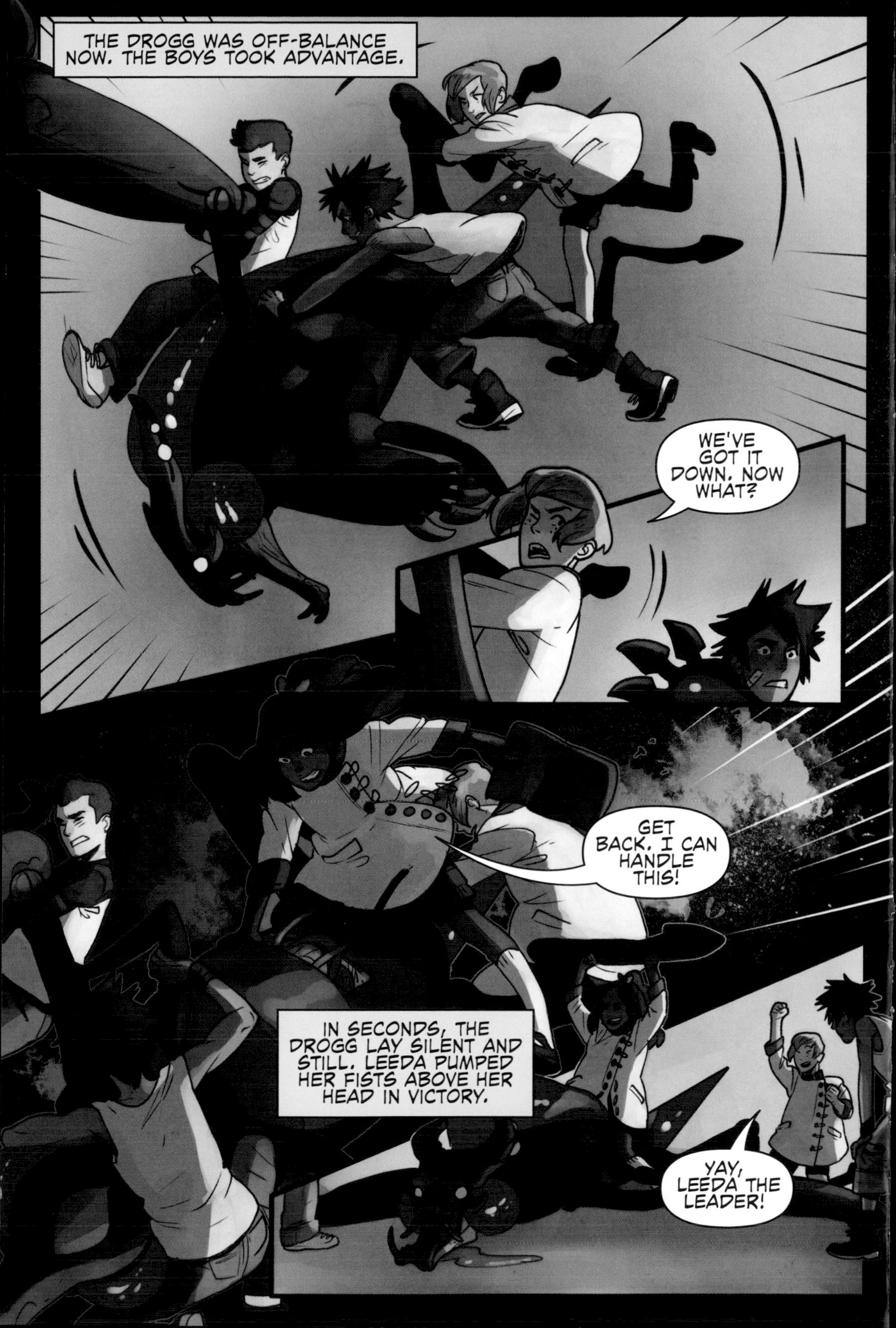
THE DROGG WAS OFF-BALANCE NOW. THE BOYS TOOK ADVANTAGE.
WE'VE GOT IT DOWN. NOW WHAT?
GET BACK. I CAN HANDLE THIS!
IN SECONDS, THE DROGG LAY SILENT AND STILL. LEEDA PUMPED HER FISTS ABOVE HER HEAD IN VICTORY.
YAY, LEEDA THE LEADER!

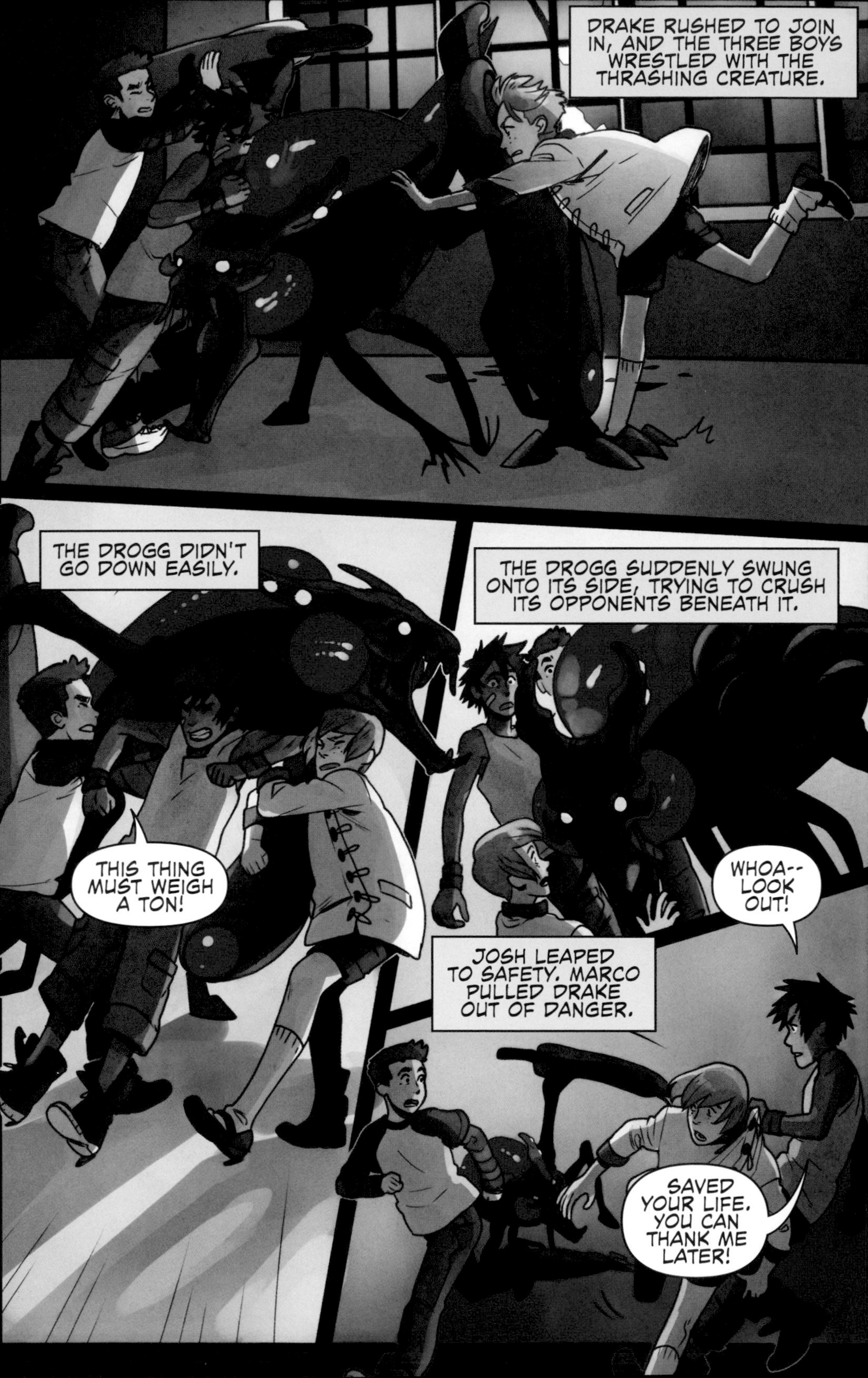
DRAKE RUSHED TO JOIN IN, AND THE THREE BOYS WRESTLED WITH THE THRASHING CREATURE.
THE DROGG DIDN'T GO DOWN EASILY.
THIS THING MUST WEIGH A TON!
THE DROGG SUDDENLY SWUNG ONTO ITS SIDE, TRYING TO CRUSH ITS OPPONENTS BENEATH IT.
WHOA-- LOOK OUT!
JOSH LEAPED TO SAFETY. MARCO PULLED DRAKE OUT OF DANGER.
SAVED YOUR LIFE. YOU CAN THANK ME LATER!

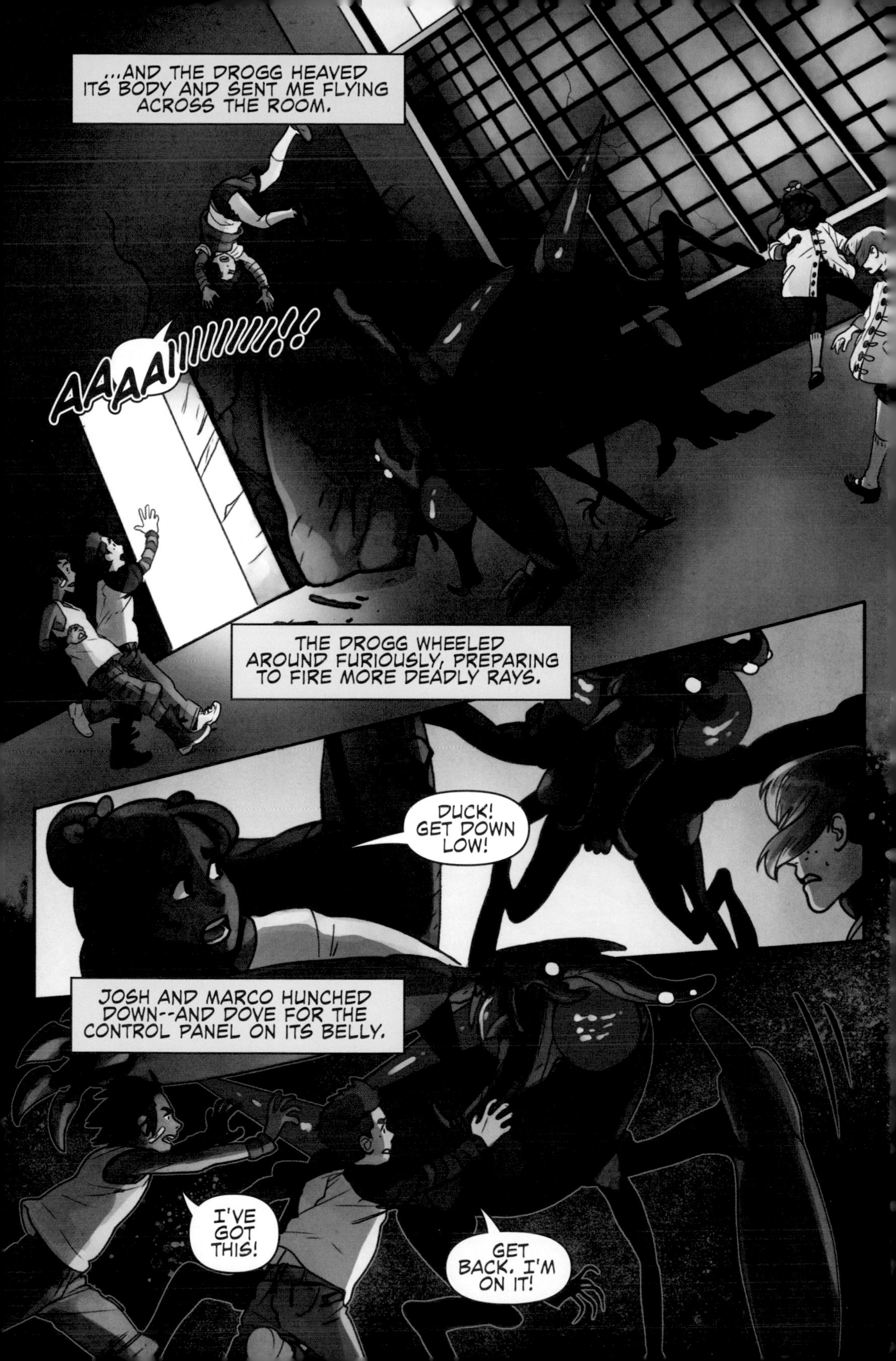
...AND THE DROGG HEAVED ITS BODY AND SENT ME FLYING ACROSS THE ROOM.
AAAAIIIIIIIIII!!
THE DROGG WHEELED AROUND FURIOUSLY, PREPARING TO FIRE MORE DEADLY RAYS.
DUCK! GET DOWN LOW!
JOSH AND MARCO HUNCHED DOWN--AND DOVE FOR THE CONTROL PANEL ON ITS BELLY.
I'VE GOT THIS!
GET BACK. I'M ON IT!

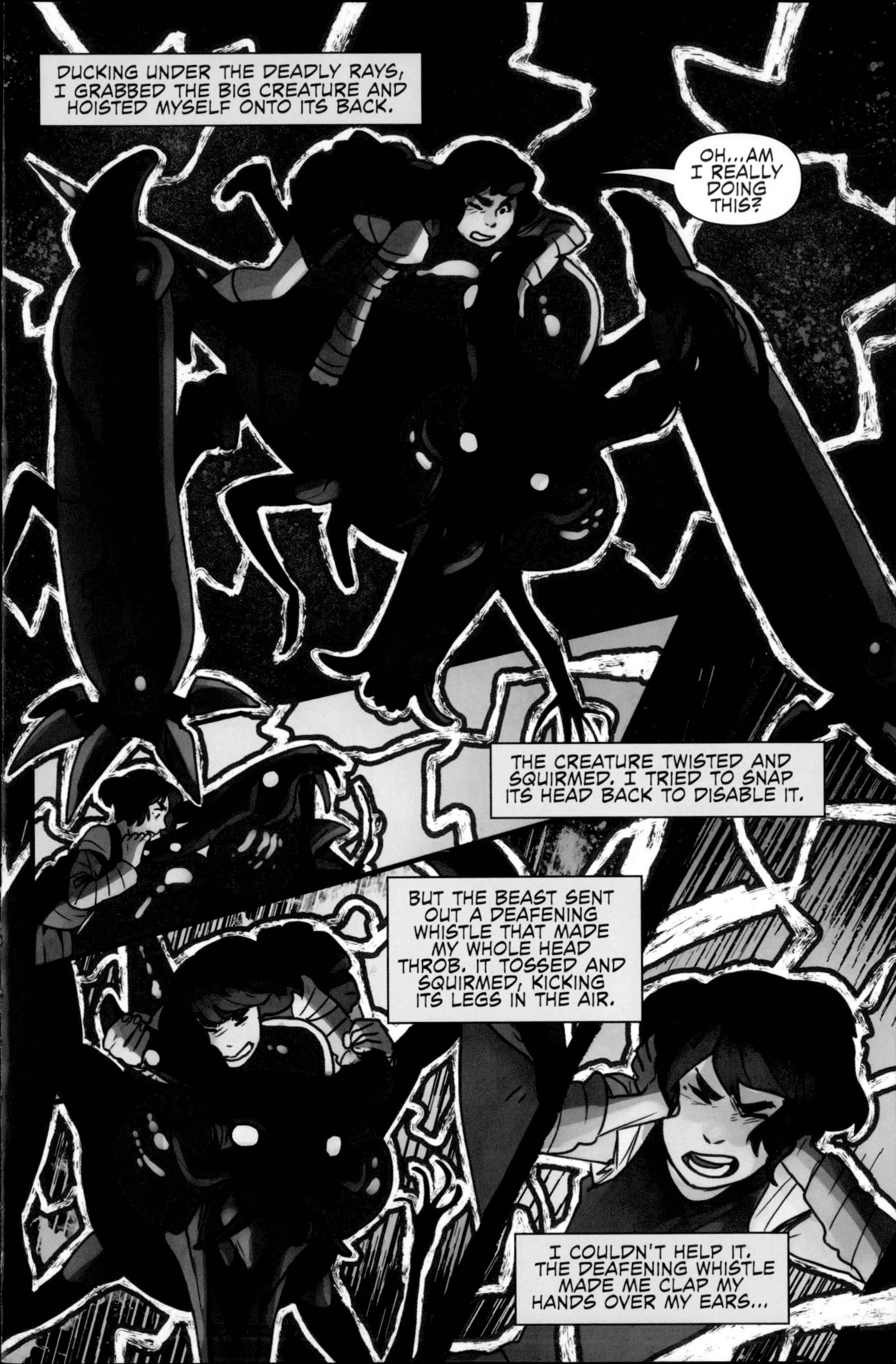
DUCKING UNDER THE DEADLY RAYS, I GRABBED THE BIG CREATURE AND HOISTED MYSELF ONTO ITS BACK.
OH...AM I REALLY DOING THIS?
THE CREATURE TWISTED AND SQUIRMED. I TRIED TO SNAP ITS HEAD BACK TO DISABLE IT.
BUT THE BEAST SENT OUT A DEAFENING WHISTLE THAT MADE MY WHOLE HEAD THROB. IT TOSSED AND SQUIRMED, KICKING ITS LEGS IN THE AIR.
I COULDN'T HELP IT. THE DEAFENING WHISTLE MADE ME CLAP MY HANDS OVER MY EARS...

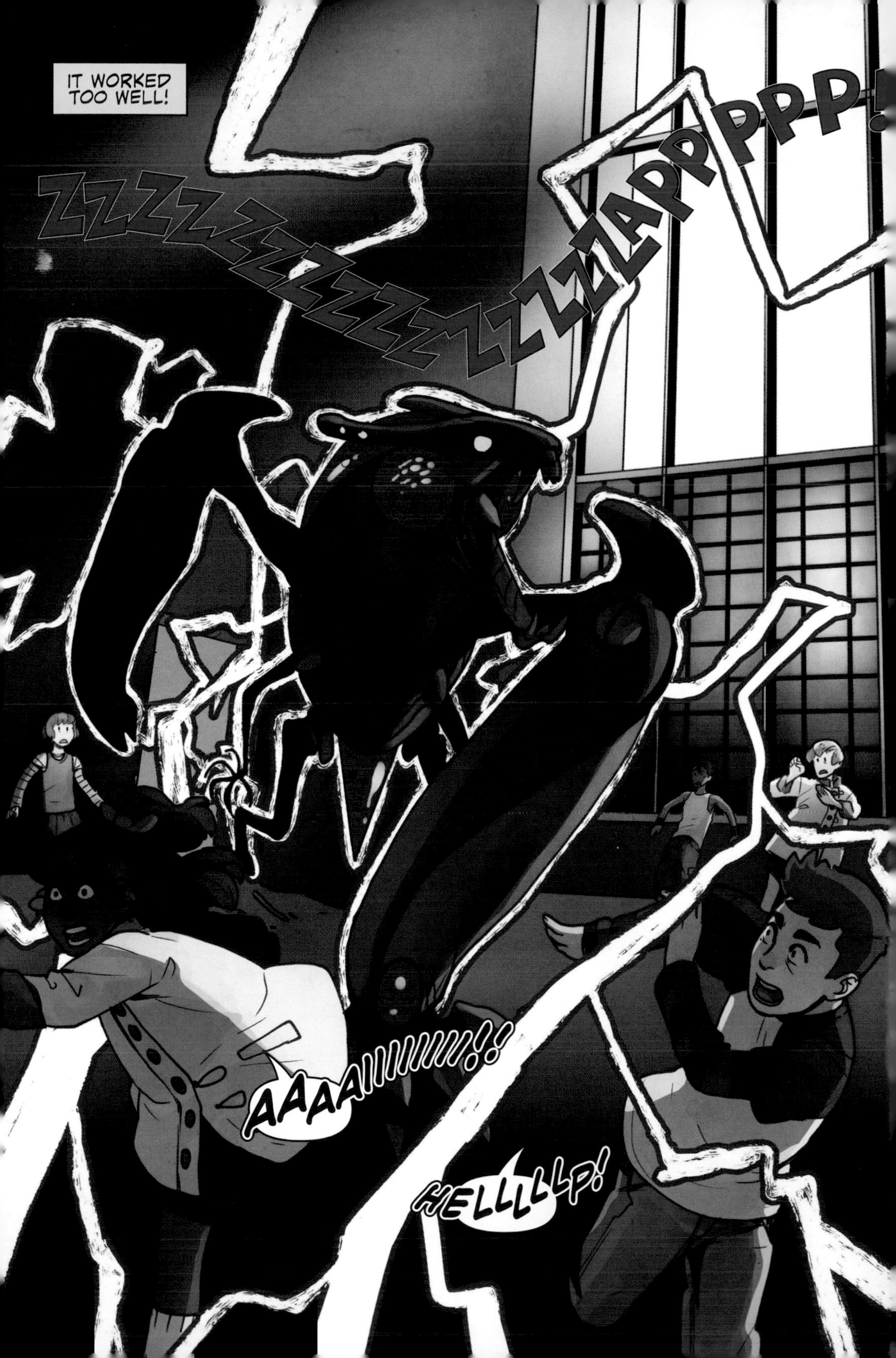
IT WORKED TOO WELL!
ZZZZZZZZZZZZZZZZZZZAPPPPPP!
AAAAIIIIIIIIIII!!
HELLLLLP!

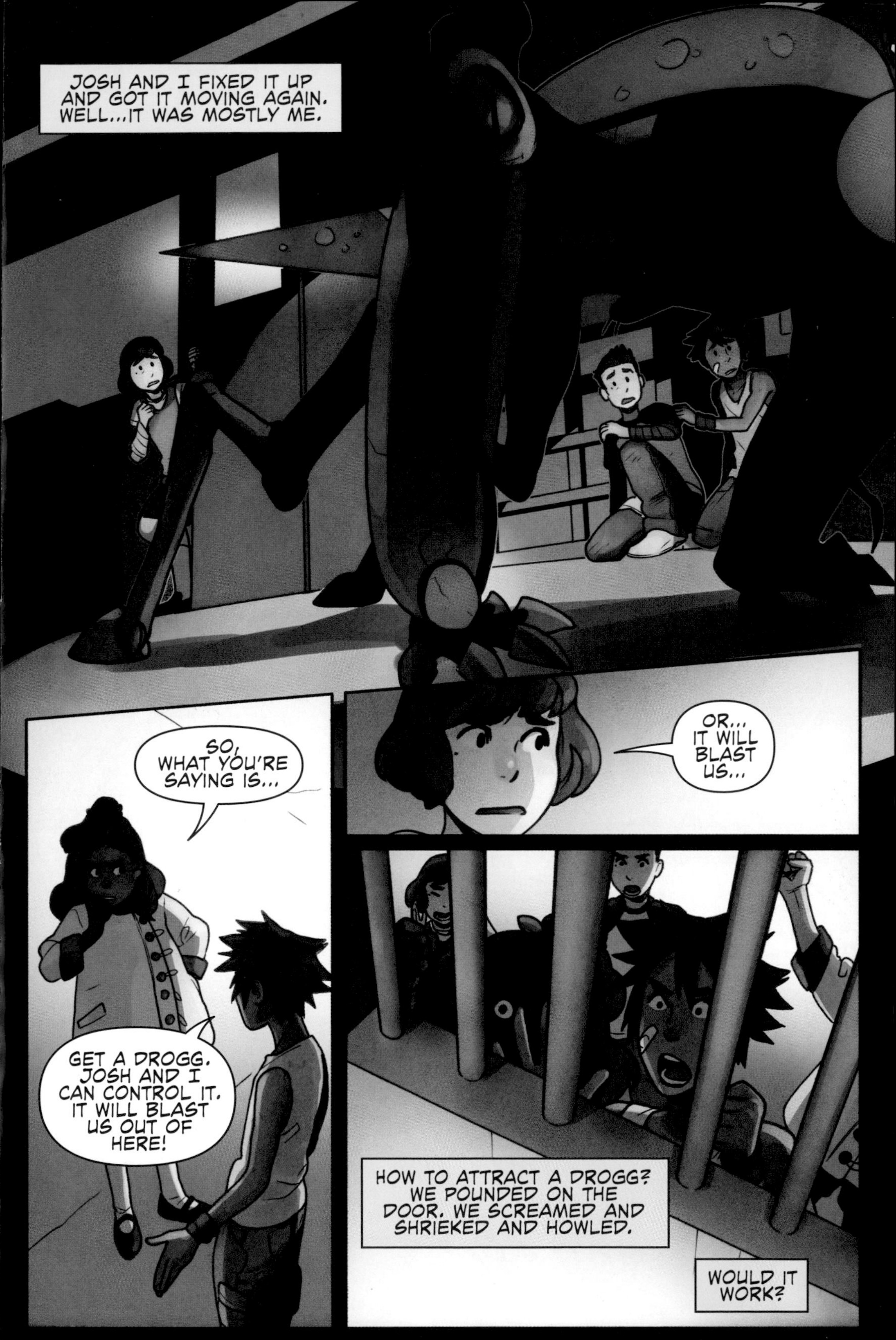
JOSH AND I FIXED IT UP AND GOT IT MOVING AGAIN. WELL...IT WAS MOSTLY ME.
SO, WHAT YOU'RE SAYING IS...
GET A DROGG. JOSH AND I CAN CONTROL IT. IT WILL BLAST US OUT OF HERE!
OR... IT WILL BLAST US...
HOW TO ATTRACT A DROGG? WE POUNDED ON THE DOOR. WE SCREAMED AND SHRIEKED AND HOWLED.
WOULD IT WORK?

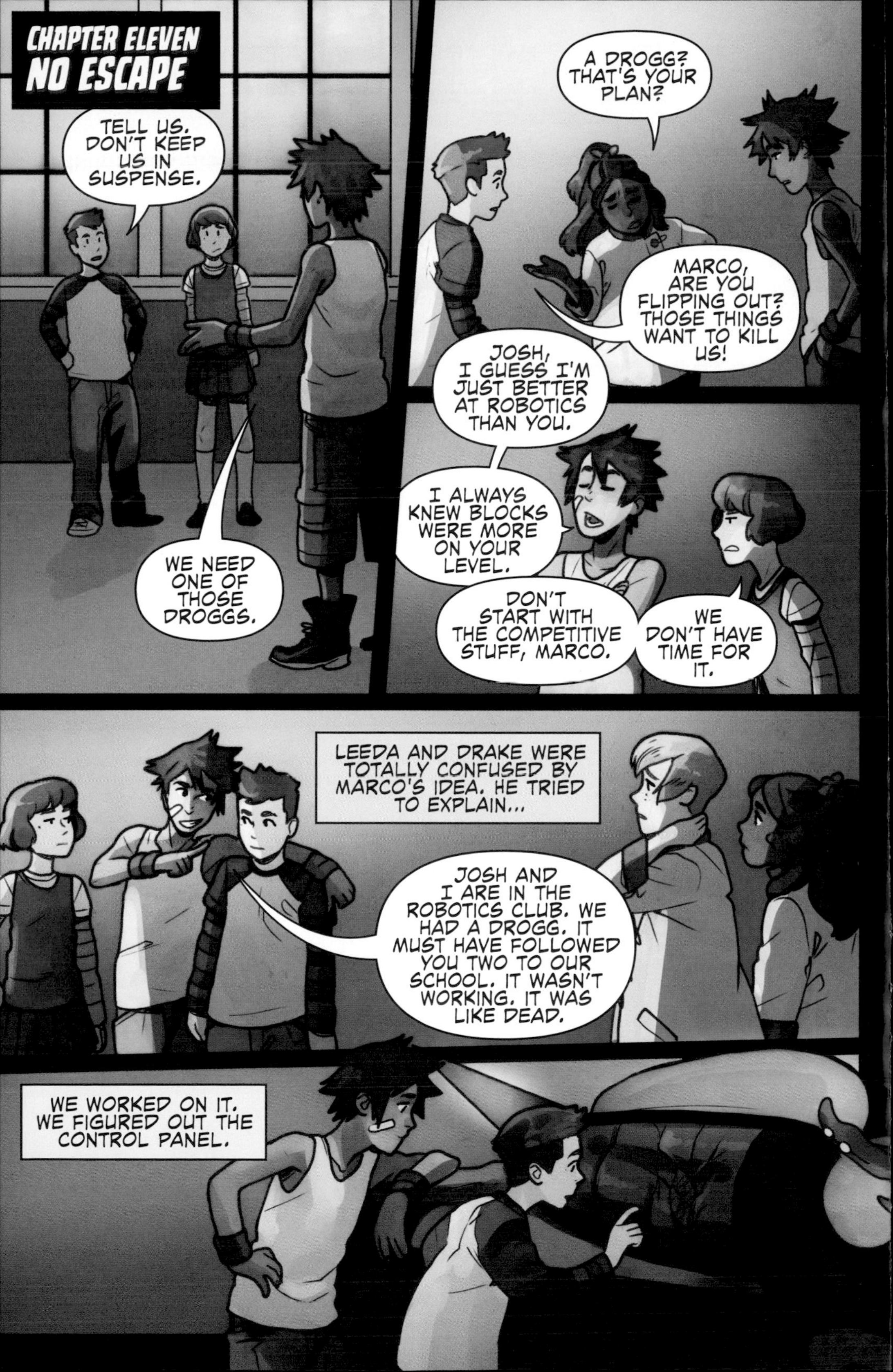
CHAPTER ELEVEN
NO ESCAPE
TELL US. DON'T KEEP US IN SUSPENSE.
WE NEED ONE OF THOSE DROGGS.
A DROGG? THAT'S YOUR PLAN?
MARCO, ARE YOU FLIPPING OUT? THOSE THINGS WANT TO KILL US!
JOSH, I GUESS I'M JUST BETTER AT ROBOTICS THAN YOU.
I ALWAYS KNEW BLOCKS WERE MORE ON YOUR LEVEL.
DON'T START WITH THE COMPETITIVE STUFF, MARCO.
WE DON'T HAVE TIME FOR IT.
LEEDA AND DRAKE WERE TOTALLY CONFUSED BY MARCO'S IDEA. HE TRIED TO EXPLAIN...
JOSH AND I ARE IN THE ROBOTICS CLUB. WE HAD A DROGG. IT MUST HAVE FOLLOWED YOU TWO TO OUR SCHOOL. IT WASN'T WORKING. IT WAS LIKE DEAD.
WE WORKED ON IT. WE FIGURED OUT THE CONTROL PANEL.

JUST BEYOND™

VOLUME 4: NO ESCAPE

Written by
R.L. Stine

Illustrated by
Kelly & Nichole Matthews

Lettered by
Mike Fiorentino

Cover by
Miguel Mercado

Just Beyond created by
R.L. Stine

Designer
Scott Newman

Assistant Editor
Michael Moccio

Editors
Whitney Leopard & Bryce Carlson

ABDOBOOKS.COM

Reinforced library bound edition published in 2021 by Spotlight, a division of ABDO, PO Box 398166, Minneapolis, Minnesota 55439. Spotlight produces high-quality reinforced library bound editions for schools and libraries. Published by agreement with KaBOOM!

Printed in the United States of America, North Mankato, Minnesota.
042020 092020

kaboom!™

JUST BEYOND: THE SCARE SCHOOL, September 2021. Published by KaBOOM!, a division of Boom Entertainment, Inc.

BOOM! Studios, 5670 Wilshire Boulevard, Suite 400, Los Angeles, CA 90036-5679.

Library of Congress Control Number: 2019955624

THIS BOOK CONTAINS RECYCLED MATERIALS

Publisher's Cataloging-in-Publication Data

Names: Stine, R.L., author. | Matthews, Kelly; Matthews, Nichole, illustrators.
Title: No escape / by R.L. Stine; illustrated by Kelly Matthews, and Nichole Matthews.
Description: Minneapolis, Minnesota: Spotlight, 2021. | Series: Just beyond; volume 4
Summary: Jess, Josh, Marco, Leeda, and Drake come up with a plan to escape the scare school and avoid the master dean's clutches.
Identifiers: ISBN 9781532144929 (lib. bdg.)
Subjects: LCSH: Middle school students--Juvenile fiction. | School buildings--Juvenile fiction. | Monsters--Juvenile fiction. | Supernatural--Juvenile fiction. | Fear--Juvenile fiction. | Graphic novels--Juvenile fiction.
Classification: DDC 741.5--dc23

[illegible] Division of ABDO
abdobooks.com